Our Little Brazilian Cousin

By

Mary F. Nixon-Roulet

Our Little Brazilian Cousin

CHAPTER I

A QUIET SIESTA

AFFONZO was tired of talking to the white cockatoo. It was the time of day when his little sister Lola took her siesta, and he had no one to play with. He was himself such a big boy, soon eleven years old, that he felt no longer the need of the daily siesta, although in the warm country of Brazil where he lived, even grown people like a nap in the middle of the day.

Affonzo himself did not feel very lively. The sun beat down like a great ball of fire and only the cool veranda or the shady garden seemed enticing. The garden should have been pleasant enough to satisfy any boy, for it was a vision of tropic beauty. Tall palms waved their feathery branches heavenward, and gaily coloured flowers flaunted their gorgeous petals while brilliant birds flittered hither and yon.

But Affonzo was used to all this beauty, and he wanted something new to do, for this little Brazilian cousin was very like his American ones and could not be quiet very long. Even the fruit garden seemed tiresome. Generally he was glad to spend his time there, for the huge banana trees which grew in a banana patch at the end of the house were sure of several visits from him during the day. The plants were twice as tall as he, and the fruit grew in great bunches, many of them weighing fifty pounds, and Affonzo always chose the finest for himself and Lola to eat. Besides these there were figs, pineapples, mangoes, grapes and oranges all of which grow in Brazil.

The American watermelon also had been planted and the Senhor was watching eagerly to see if it would bear fruit, for he had been told that in other parts of Brazil it grew rapidly and bore well. Affonzo was much interested in it too, for his cousin in the States had sent the seeds and told him how delicious the fruit was.

He strolled toward the sunny slope where the vines were tended by Joachim, the black who took care of the garden and helped about the house. Joachim's mother had nursed Affonzo's mother in the days when there were black slaves in Brazil, and he was devoted to the whole family. He was just like a faithful black dog watching the place, and was especially fond of the children. He could cook and bake, wait on the Senhor, tend the garden or the horses, and could always be trusted to take care of little Lola who was his great friend.

Affonzo looked at the green melon and wondered how it tasted. He had heard so much about it that he was very curious and could hardly wait until the day came when it should be served, for his mother had promised that each should have a taste.

Above the melon vines grew one of the tallest of the banana trees, and the fruit seemed to Affonzo to be finer at that particular time than he had ever seen it. He was very hungry and felt he must have one of those bananas at once. Ordinarily he would have climbed the tree like a little monkey and helped himself, but his mother had excused him from his siesta on condition that he be quiet, and though he looked longingly at the fruit he did not start to climb. He threw himself down upon the grass and looked up through the thick foliage at the blue above.

"I wish something would happen," he said to himself. "It seems to me that nothing ever happens. One half the year I must be in Para and stay at my grandfather's to go to the Laure Sodré Institute—I am tired of the very name!—and the other half I must stay here at the Fazenda with no playmate but Lola, and she is made to sleep half the day. I wish something would happen," and he sighed discontentedly. "How hungry I am," he thought. "I must have one of those bananas, they never looked so good! I believe mamma will not care if I climb for one, for she only said I must keep quiet and I'm sure I'll make no noise." With that the boy rose to his feet, and with a quick glance around, he began to climb and was soon squirming around the trunk of the tree like a snake. Once there he reached for the best bananas and filled the pockets of his linen suit with them. He was just starting down when he heard voices coming and peering cautiously down the garden path he saw his father with an uncle of whom he was very fond, and whom he had not seen for some time.

"Uncle Prudente," he thought. "I wonder when he came from Para and how long he is going to stay. Oh, dear! how will I get down from here?" Affonzo knew that his father would not be likely to pass over any disobedience and that he would be punished if he came down at that moment. So he crouched among the leaves and was still as a mouse while the two gentlemen came directly under the banana tree and stopped to talk.

"This is the American melon," said the Senhor. "It will be ripe in another week. There are others ripening but this is the finest. If it is good I shall keep all the seeds and have a large crop next year. If Juan comes, I shall ask him to bring me the seeds of various kinds, for there is nothing like variety in a garden. In our hot climate these should do well and they are very agreeable when properly cooled. I hope Juan will come; a long visit from him would be a good thing for Affonzo, who is growing spoiled from being the only boy. He is wilful and high-spirited but on the whole he is—what is that?"

The Senhor stopped suddenly and Affonzo never knew what he himself was, besides being wilful and high spirited. Distressed at being a listener, he had leaned too far out on the branch on which he sat and it broke under his weight. He gave a wild clutch and fell down, down, down. He thought he would never stop, and oh, horror! when he did light, it was astride the shoulders of his uncle. Affonzo was a sturdy little fellow and his uncle was slight and small, the result being that both went down in a heap on top of the melon.

For a moment no one spoke; then his father pulled him off his uncle and helped his irate brother to his feet. Uncle Prudente's white linen suit was splashed from head to foot with watermelon juice, his panama hat was crushed out of shape, watermelon juice ran down his face and several black seeds stuck to his face. He was speechless with rage, but he looked so very funny that Affonzo, sore and bruised by his fall and terribly frightened, could not help laughing. He sat down upon the ground and laughed till he cried, and the noise woke all the parrots dozing in the trees, and all began jabbering at once, while the cockatoo gave one of his terrible screeches.

When the noise had subsided a little, Senhor Dias said sternly to Affonzo, "What is the meaning of this?" Affonzo was silent, but he quickly sprang to his feet and stood respectfully in front of his father, for Brazilian boys are taught to treat their elders with great deference.

"What were you doing in that tree?" demanded his father.

"Eating bananas," said Affonzo simply.

"Does your mother permit that?" asked the Senhor, for in Brazil, as in most South American countries, the mother arranges all matters in regard to the children.

"My mother allows me to climb trees and eat bananas," said Affonzo. "That was not a disobedience, but—"

"But what?" demanded his father.

"But," continued Affonzo slowly. "She had at the hour of the siesta requested me to keep quiet."

"Do you call this quiet?" asked his father sternly though his eyes twinkled. "Such a noise has not been heard at the Fazenda for many days."

"Not very quiet," said Affonzo, his head drooping, though he could scarce keep from laughing again. "I ask your pardon, my uncle," he added. "I intended nothing of disrespect. I did but lose my hold upon the tree and the next thing I knew I sat astride of your august shoulders. I pray you pardon me." Affonzo's tone was contrite, and his dancing eyes were on the ground.

"Say no more of it," said his uncle, as he laid his hand on the boy's head. "Boys will be boys and Affonzo is not unlike others. But next time I come do not receive me with such a fierce embrace. Indeed I thought my neck was broken with the warmth of your welcome."

Affonzo's laugh rang out gaily, but he sobered down when his father said, "I excuse you since your uncle asks it, but remember after this that the commands of your mother are to be obeyed. Go now with your uncle and attend to his wants while he repairs the damage your carelessness has wrought."

Affonzo bowed to his father and made the military salute as all school boys are taught to do in Brazil, but he sighed to himself as he went, "I wonder what he meant about Juan but I am afraid to ask. And the worst of it all is, that now I shall never know how the American melon tasted."

CHAPTER II

IN THE FOREST

THE sun was just rising and its slanting rays cast a golden glow over the thick foliage when Affonzo sprang out of bed next morning, awakened by the noisy chattering of the birds.

"Hurrah!" he exclaimed. "It is a fine day! How glad I am, for now I can go hunting with my father and Uncle Prudente."

He hurried into his clothes and down to the breakfast-room, where Joachim was serving strong black coffee, rolls and fruit to his father and uncle.

"Here you are, bright and early," said the Senhor. "Do you want to go with us? Perhaps you would better not!"

Affonzo's face fell.

"Oh, father! last night you promised!" he said, and his father answered, "Oh, you may go. I merely thought perhaps it might tire you too much, for we shall have a long tramp."

"We must start at once," said his uncle, "if we are to have any sport before midday," and they started toward the forest.

The Fazenda of the Senhor Dias was situated on the edge of the magnificent woods which line the banks of the Amazon near the City of Para.

"No wonder that this region around Para is called the Paradise of Brazil," said the Senhor as they entered the forest, where heavy dew glittered on the leaves like diamonds in an emerald crown. "Every time I enter the forest it seems to me more splendid than it did the last time."

"What are those huge trees?" asked Affonzo.

"You ought to know those, for they are among the most famous of all Brazilian trees. They are the Stanba or stone wood, and beside them grows a cinnamon tree. In addition to these there is the jacaranda, pas d' arc, the euphorbia, the large lofty cotton-wood tree, the tall white syringa."

"I know that one," said Affonzo. "It is a rubber tree. Won't you take me to see the rubber gathered to-day?"

"Not to-day, but to-morrow, perhaps, for your uncle wishes to make the rounds and you may go with him."

"Thank you, that will be delightful," said Affonzo.

Their path led through the forest where long racemes of tropic moss hung down and waved in the breeze, while fern and vines grew in a tangle across the narrow path. Often the undergrowth was so thick, that Joachim had to go before the party and cut it away with histracado.

"You must keep silent now," said the Senhor.

"We shall frighten the game away if we talk. Ah!" As he spoke he raised his gun to his shoulder and fired. There was a shrill cry, a flash of red and green wings, and a large bird with an enormous bill fluttered to the ground before them.

"A toucan!" cried Affonzo, as Joachim quickly bagged the bird. "Isn't it queer that the bird's cry sounded just like its name, Toucano! Toucano!"

"That is just the reason that the Indians named them toucano," said the Senhor. "But listen, I hear monkeys."

Looking carefully about, the hunters saw two monkeys at the top of a high tree, about which clung a monkey's ladder, an enormous vine which wound around the tree from its roots to its very topmost branches. When the little animals saw that they were perceived, they tried to conceal themselves behind the huge leaves of the tree, and the Senhor's shot showed no result beyond an increased chattering.

"It seems a shame to kill such cunning little creatures," said Affonzo, but his father said,

"We hunt for food, not for mere sport, my son. Monkeys make an excellent dinner, and you will be glad enough to eat after we have tramped all morning through the heat."

"Master will not hit the monkeys," said Joachim. "I will get them," and he quickly stripped off all his clothing, except his cotton trousers, and began to climb the monkey ladder.

It was not easy to climb with his gun in one hand but he was careful and as nimble as a cat, and he soon neared the top of the tree. He perched in a crotch of the tree, which branched out thickly at the top, and hiding behind some leaves he waited until he could get a glimpse of the monkeys. At last he spied one of them at the end of a branch and firing quickly, the monkey fell to the ground, fifty feet below.

Joachim climbed down after it and the party soon went its way through the forest. Now the Senhor shot, and then his brother, and the boy himself was allowed to fire at an ocelot which crept through the bushes, and great was his delight when he shot it.

As the noon hour approached, the sun rose high in the heavens, and the heat grew so intense that the Senhor said,

"We will go no farther. Let us rest and eat until it grows cooler. Joachim, lead us to a shady spot where we may camp."

"Yes, Senhor," said the black, and soon he brought them to a ruined building of stone, covered with vines and hidden among the trees. Here upon the stone floor of the ruin, he kindled a fire and cooked the monkey, the flesh of which was simply delicious, and Affonzo ate until he was so sleepy that he could not keep his eyes open.

"What was this building?" he asked his father. "I did not know anyone had ever lived here."

"No one knows what it was," replied his father. "It has been here for years and the Indians say it was built many, many years ago by a Black Gown, as they called the early missionaries. It may have been the beginning of a mission house, but in any case it makes a very nice cool place in which to take our siesta now. So sleep, my son, and wake refreshed."

Affonzo closed his eyes and was soon in dreamland. He slept long but had strange dreams of some one's putting a heavy stone upon his chest and pressing it down. At last he awoke with the pressure still on him. He lay quite still, drowsily wondering what was the matter with him and before he stirred, Joachim's voice said in a hoarse whisper,

"Don't move, little master, don't even open your eyes!"

Affonzo had been trained to habits of strictest obedience, and he lay perfectly still without moving a muscle, although wondering very much what was the matter. He heard Joachim dart quickly to his side. There was the sound of a blow, and a loud exclamation from his father, and Joachim said,

"Jump up, there is no danger now!"

As Affonzo sprang to his feet, the weight rolled off his chest, and he saw the body of a large snake pinned to the earth by the blade of Joachim's trocado. It was a jararaca, a Brazilian snake about six feet long, of a yellowish colour. Sleeping in the cool of the old stone ruin it had been disturbed by the intruders, and had crawled across Affonzo's body to reach the door.

"My boy, you have Joachim to thank for saving your life," said his father warmly, as he put his arm around his boy and drew him to his side. "The jararaca is very poisonous, and had your awakening disturbed him, he might have driven his fangs into you."

"Good old Joachim," said Affonzo, as he threw his arms around the black's neck. Negro servants in Brazil who have been in a family for years are always much beloved, and Affonzo was devoted to the old negro. Joachim didn't say much, but smiled at the boy as he took the dead body of the snake outside, and prepared to take off its beautiful skin.

CHAPTER III
A TROPICAL STORM

"What fortunes could be made in these forests," said the Senhor Dias to his brother, "if people with capital only knew of the riches stored here. Mahogany, satinwood, rosewood and many other kinds of trees grow here in the greatest abundance, and were there railroads and ships to transport them, Brazil would be one of the richest countries in the world."

"We should try to develop our own land," said his brother, and the two men entered into a long conversation as to the wonderful forests of the country, to which Affonzo listened with interest.

"Oh, father!" he exclaimed, at last. "When you go up the river to see the forests may I go with you?"

"Perhaps, but I could not make a promise without first asking your mother's consent. The trip will be an interesting one, but very hard, though it might do you good."

"I should love to go," said Affonzo, and his uncle added, "He will grow up a milksop if you keep him in the nursery much longer; let him go."

"It is about time we were starting now," said the Senhor. "Joachim, make ready the bag. Your uncle and I will walk on a little ahead, Affonzo, and you can follow with Joachim. But do not stray away from him, or you will miss the path, and all manner of dangers lurk in these forests."

Affonzo sat lazily waiting and watching as the black put up the dinner things. "Take care of my snake skin," he said, and Joachim smiled, and replied, "That will make a fine belt for the little master when it is dried."

"I should like that very much," said Affonzo. "You must make it for me."

"Yes, sir," said Joachim as he swung over his strong shoulders the wickerwork hamper and game bag. "Is the young master ready to go?"

"I am," Affonzo replied, and the two started down the narrow path along which the Senhor had disappeared.

"What kind of a tree is that?" asked Affonzo pointing to a tall tree a hundred feet high.

"That is the castanhao," said Joachim. "Some people call it the Brazil nut, and I have often gathered nuts from it for you to eat. The nuts grow at the very top of the tree in shells like cocoanuts, and each shell has fifteen or twenty nuts in it. Often I have thought my head was broken when a shell fell upon it."

"I wonder why we don't catch up with my father?" said Affonzo. "Joachim, what makes it so dark?"

"Storm coming. We must hurry," was the brief answer.

Heavy clouds had gathered quickly; not a glimmer of sunlight came through the trees, and great drops of rain began to fall.

"Father!" cried Affonzo, but there was no answer. "Father!" he called again and Joachim shouted, "Senhor! Senhor!"

Nothing was heard but the screaming of the wind, and the rain fell faster and faster. Vivid flashes of lightning illuminated the forest, and the thunder muttered and grumbled in the distance.

"Come with me quickly," said Joachim, as he seized the boy by the hand. "We mustn't stay here."

"But my father," cried Affonzo and tried to get away from Joachim, but the negro held tight to him.

"The Senhor can take care of himself; I must take care of you," he said, as he pulled the boy into a side path which led through the woods. They made their way with difficulty through the dense tangle of underbrush and vines. Often a swinging branch would strike Affonzo on the face, or he would tangle his feet in a swaying vine and fall full length in a bed of fern. The rain poured down in torrents, but the leaves and interlaced branches served as a shield from the great drops which pelted down like bullets. Soon they came to a small hut with a thatched roof and no door to bar the entrance. Into it Joachim pulled the boy with scant ceremony. As they entered the hut a man rose hurriedly from his grass couch, and Affonzo recognized an Indian who had often been to the Fazenda to see his father.

"Ah, Vicente," said Joachim. "Give us shelter."

"Welcome," said the syringuero. "The storm is bad. You reached shelter just in time. See!"

He pointed through the door-way and Affonzo saw that the streams of water were well-nigh rivers, and the thunder and lightning were almost incessant.

"Where do you suppose my father is?" he asked, and Joachim answered,

"The Senhor has found shelter, do not fear; and he will know you are safe with me."

"There is nothing to do but sit still, I suppose," said Affonzo, rather mournfully, for that was the hardest thing in all the world for him to do.

Vicente gave him a slow smile. He was an old Indian of wiry frame, with keen black eyes. His hair was straight and black, his chin firm and strong, his features clean-cut, his face proud and intelligent. He was in great contrast to curly-haired, black Joachim with his good-humoured, stolid face.

Vicente was one of the Indians whose fathers had owned the land before the Portuguese discovered it and named it Brazil from the red colour of its dye woods. He gathered rubber from the great trees which grew in the forest, and lived alone in his little hut. He sat smoking and watching the boy who looked out into the rain feeling very miserable.

"Vicente," he said at last, "have you lived long in the forest?"

"Many years have I been here," said the old man. "And my fathers were here before me. They hunted and fished and were chiefs in the land until the white men came. Many died, many went to the great hills, but I stayed here, for the home of my fathers is my home."

"Tell me a story, Vicente," begged the little boy.

"In the days of my fathers," said Vicente, "and of my father's fathers and their fathers, things were not as to-day they are in the country of the great river. There were no white Senhores. The Indians dwelt alone. They roamed the forests hunting with the bow and arrow; they fished in the great stream; they dwelt in their lodges and were happy.

"Often there were fights with other Indians and these were of great glory. But my people were peaceful and loved not war, never fighting if they could first have peace. To secure peace for our village, each year they made a sacrifice and this was the manner of it.

"A chief smeared his body with gum and then powdered himself with gold dust. He powdered it all over, for in our mountains was much gold and precious gems. He placed himself on a raft and was rowed to the middle of the great river. There he raised his hands to heaven, praying the Great Spirit to save his village, and jumping into the water he washed off the precious dust. This he sacrificed for his village.

"This was done each year and should have been done still, when, perhaps, the Indian villages would not have been destroyed and deserted, but it ceased for the sin of one man. A chief loved gold. That is an evil and a foolishness, for gold is but for use and not for love. He loved its glitter, and it seemed to him stupid to waste it in a sacrifice.

"It was his turn to make the river sacrifice and become the Gilded Man. But he was angry within himself, and said, 'why shall I do this thing? If the village wishes gold, why must it take mine? It is a foolish thing!'

"Yet he could not refuse the sacrifice, for to be the Gilded Man was thought an honour, and did he refuse, many would suspect him of faithlessness to his tribe. So he gilded himself as was the custom, and his brother chiefs rowed him to the river and he raised his hands to heaven.

"'Spirits of Rain and Wind, of Fire and Water, of Good and Evil, keep our village and our people,' he cried. 'We offer all to thee!' Then he plunged into the stream and washed the gold from his arms and legs. All the time his heart was hot within him and he thought to himself, 'How my soul grieves to see this waste of the beautiful, shining dust!' Then an evil spirit tempted him and he did not wash off all the gold. He left beneath his arms where others could not see it, some of the glittering dust, and returned to his village, an insult to the Spirits of Heaven.

"That night came fierce rain and wind and with it a horde of enemies who descended like a hurricane and destroyed the village,—men, women and children. So the chief with all his gold was destroyed utterly and he was the last Gilded Man. Thus were the Spirits of Heaven avenged!"

"Thank you, Vicente," cried Affonzo. "That is a good story. But see, the rain is over. Now we must hurry to find my father," pointing as he spoke to the doorway. The sky was clear and bright, already rose-tinted with the rays of the setting sun, low in the heavens.

"You must not go yet," said Vicente. "Ground too wet, trees wet, bad for white people. You must wait."

"But I must find my father," persisted Affonzo, who, though he was a brave boy, began to be somewhat frightened. But Vicente knew the danger of the steaming forest with its snakes, mosquitoes and insects swarming after the storm. "Not safe to go now," he said, and Joachim, who was quite comfortable where he was, said, "Little master must sleep here and go home in the morning."

"You shall have a good supper," said Vicente, who began at once to prepare the meal, and Affonzo was forced to submit. So he watched with interest the preparations for supper, for like most boys, he was generally hungry. Vicente built a fire in the stone fireplace in front of his hut, and from a stone jar in the corner he brought pork, some coarse bread, wild honey found in the woods, and bananas.

"Take a bird from our bag," said Affonzo, wishing to give his share of the feast, and Joachim brought out a parrot which was soon stewing in the pot with the pork, and a handful of peppers and herbs. When the savoury stew was done, the meal was spread upon a rough bench at the door, and the three odd companions sat down together.

"Quite a festive party," said a laughing voice, and jumping up, Affonzo saw his father and uncle approaching through the trees.

"Oh, papa, how glad I am to see you! I feared you would be wet through, but you must have found shelter as we did, for you are scarcely wet at all."

"I worried about you, more than you did about me, I fancy," said his father, "though I hoped Joachim would bring you here. Your uncle and I missed the path some way, and could not find you or the old house again, so we took refuge in a deserted hut."

"The Senhors will sup with me," said Vicente, "and remain here for the night since the forest is unsafe for the boy."

"A thousand thanks; we will stay if you can arrange for so many," was the reply, and as Vicente assured them that they would all be most welcome, they ate their supper with much enjoyment.

The two Senhors slept in Indian hammocks swung between giant rubber trees, while Affonzo curled up in a blanket and slept, as did Vicente and Joachim, on a fragrant couch of dried grass.

CHAPTER IV
ALONG THE AMAZON

"COME, son," said the Senhor early next morning. "We have a long day before us and you must eat plenty of breakfast. That is if you want to go with your uncle and me. If not, you may go back home with Joachim."

"Where are you going?" asked Affonzo as he smoothed down his linen suit, and combed his hair with a pocket comb from his dapper little uncle's case. He had washed his face in the stream which gurgled near the hut, and that was all the toilet he could make, which seemed odd to him, for he was something of a dandy.

"We are going the rounds with Vicente to see the rubber plantation, and then go home by the river."

"Do let me go with you, I am sure my mother would not object," cried Affonzo.

"I shall send Joachim home with word of your safety to ease her mind, and as you wish it so much, you may come with us; so eat and we will start."

Senhor Dias was a rubber exporter. From his plantation near Para went out huge balls of the rubber, solid, tough and brown. It is very interesting to watch the process of obtaining this from the milk-white sap of the rubber trees.

"Well, Vicente, shall we start now," said the Senhor when they had breakfasted.

"When the Senhor is ready," said Vicente.

The Indian lived by himself all the year around in his little hut. All along the Amazon these cabins may be found, hidden in the woods, and in each one dwells only a single Indian. It is a lonely and dangerous life, the climate is unhealthful, the swampy lands of the river valley where the rubber trees grow are low and malarious, and the syringuero has often to wade knee deep in mud, and work all day in wet clothing.

The Indians are trustworthy workers and many of them earn a good living. Old Vicente had worked there so long that he would not have known how to act anywhere else, but he was glad to have company on his lonely rounds. So he smiled at Affonzo as the boy skipped along, gathering one gorgeous flower after another, as merry as the sunshine after the rain.

"You'd better walk a little more slowly, and save your strength for the day's tramp," said his father. "You'll be tired by night."

Vicente guided them down a well-worn path through the marsh land. On each side were splendid trees, the rubber tree growing as high as seventy feet. The trunk, smooth and round, was covered with light-coloured bark, the leaves, oval and about a foot long, hanging in clusters of three. The fruit grows in clusters also, and consists of a small black nut which the natives like very much. Affonzo picked one up and tasted it, but made a very wry face as it was quite bitter.

Selecting a fine tree, Vicente made a deep cut in the bark with his hatchet. Below it, by means of some damp clay, he fastened an earthen cup, into which the cream-coloured sap flowed slowly.

"By to-morrow the cup will be full," he said. "And I will come again. Now we will find another."

The next tree was half a mile away and it had frequently been tapped before, for a row of incisions girdled it. Vicente emptied the cups attached to these into a large pail which he carried, and made a new gash higher up.

"Do let me tap just one tree," said Affonzo, and Vicente allowed him to do so and helped him fasten on one of the cups to catch the sap. Affonzo was delighted, and tramped along gaily, although his short legs found it difficult to keep up with the long strides of his father and uncle.

At last Vicente finished his rounds, and said, as he showed the Senhor his brimming pail, "This is all to-day. Does the Senhor wish to see it cooked?"

"Yes, I want Affonzo to see it all, as I know he will be interested," said Senhor Dias, and they all followed the Indian to a little hut, such as the one in which they had slept the night before.

"Let us eat first," said the Senhor. "Our walk has given us all appetites."

So Vicente built a fire and roasted a lagarto which he had killed on the way through the forest. The delicate white flesh tasted delicious to Affonzo, and so did the bananas and oranges and black coffee, which Vicente made thick and strong as it is liked in Brazil.

Vicente then made another fire of nuts and the wood of the motacu under a jug-shaped calabash, the smoke coming out through the neck. This smoke hastens the drying of the liquid rubber, and makes a better quality than can be obtained in any other way.

"I don't see how that stuff that looks like cream can ever be made like rubber," said Affonzo.

"Watch Vicente," said his father, "and you will see." As he spoke, Vicente dipped a long paddle into the liquid, and then held it over the smoke. It quickly dried and he dipped the paddle into the juice again, repeating the process of drying. This he kept up until the paddle had a thick coating of rubber, like a large, flattened ball. Then he split the ball open along one side, and pulled the paddle out.

"There now!" said the Senhor. "The rubber is all ready to go to market. Perhaps some day you will bounce a ball or wear a pair of goloshes made of this very rubber."

"Won't that be fine!" said Affonzo. "What are you going to do now," he asked, as his father rose as if to go.

"As soon as Vicente has finished cooking, we will go to the river, and go home by water," said the Senhor. "Then you will see some of the wood your uncle and I mean to export."

"That will be much better than tramping," said Affonzo, whose short legs began to be stiff and sore with all the walking he had done.

Vicente soon finished cooking his rubber, and put up the utensils before following Affonzo and the two men down the path to the river.

"Vicente is a good Indian, isn't he?" said Affonzo.

"One of the best I have ever known," said his father. "He has worked for us for years and has always been honest and reliable. It is strange that he should be so hospitable and friendly, for his ancestors and ours were always at war. When your grandfather was a young man there was always fear of the natives, and at one time there was an Indian uprising in which many Portuguese were killed. The Indians captured the city of Para, burned many of the houses, and destroyed everything they couldn't carry away with them. They held the city over a year before the Portuguese could recapture it."

"It must have been exciting to live then," cried Affonzo, who loved to read of wars and battles and thought they must be interesting things.

But his uncle said, "More peaceful times are less exciting, but far pleasanter and you would better be thankful that you live now. There is the river! How beautiful it looks!"

Affonzo had often seen the Amazon, the greatest river in the world, and had been on it in the steamers which ply between Para and Mañaos, but he had never seen it at this point, and he exclaimed in wonder at its beauty. The river was two miles wide, and in the centre was a broad deep channel down which the water flowed slowly. On each side of this were stretches of shallow water, while on either bank grew thick forests of superb trees.

Vicente drew a canoe from a thicket about a sheltered cove and the little party embarked, Vicente paddling carefully.

"Isn't this splendid?" cried Affonzo. "I feel as if I were Orellaño discovering the river."

"Why, what do you know about him?" asked his uncle.

"Oh, he was fine," said Affonzo. "He was one of Gonzalo Pizzarro's lieutenants and he crossed the Andes to find cinnamon trees. He had only fifty men and they built a boat and started down the river and had a terrible time for days. At last they reached the mouth of the river, and were picked up by some Spanish ships. It told all about it in my geography."

"Did it tell how he named the river?" asked Uncle Prudente. "Orellaña fell in with an Indian tribe where the women fought side by side with the men; you know women soldiers are called Amazons, so he called the river 'Rio de las Amazones.'"

"See those magnificent satin-wood trees," said Senhor Dias to his brother. "Nowhere in all the world is there such wood from which to make fine furniture as here."

Then the two gentlemen fell into a talk about business plans, and Affonzo curled up in the canoe and watched the interesting things they passed. It was a scene of contrast. A native boat, one end thatched over for a house, a hammock, in which a man lolled lazily, swung across its deck, was passing by a large steamer gay with flags and striped awnings. He also saw boats laden with rubber, and many raftsmade of great logs held together by long wooden pins driven through them, for their long voyage to Para.

As they continued down the stream, the thatched native huts became fewer, and there could be seen the tiled roofs of the country homes of the wealthy. It was not long before Affonzo saw, gleaming through the trees, the white walls of their own Fazenda and, landing quickly, he bade good-by to Vicente, and rushed across the lawn to tell all his adventures to his mother and Lola.

CHAPTER V

A VISIT TO GRANDMAMMA'S

THE Fazenda of the Senhor Dias stood upon a hill overlooking the Amazon. About it were trees and gardens, and a small stream flowed through the grounds toward the great river. A pleasant little summer-house was set under a giant palm tree and about the whole place was an air of ease and comfort. Upon the broad, pillared veranda and between the shady trees hammocks were slung for the midday siesta, and the life of the villa was cheerful and pleasant.

Affonzo was very tired the day after his jaunt through the forest, and toward evening he lazily lay in a cool hammock swinging back and forth. His sister sat on a cushion at his feet listening in delight to the story of his adventures.

Lola was only eight years old and she thought her big brother of eleven quite the most wonderful boy in the world.

"How I wish you could have been with me, Lola," said Affonzo. "Of course you could not, for girls can not go to the places that boys can. But it was most exciting! What you would like would be to hear Vicente. He told me a wonderful story."

"Do tell it to me," said Lola, and Affonzo retold the story of the Gilded Man, to her great delight.

"Oh! what a nice story," cried Lola as he finished. "What was the Indian's house like?"

"It wasn't a real house, you know," said Affonzo. "It was a little round hut all thatched with straw, and he had bows and arrows and all kinds of things." Affonzo was rather vague in his description. "The trees around were the finest I ever saw. Oh! I am sure there is no country in the world like ours!"

Lola smiled, and, touching the strings of her guitar, sang softly:

"Minha terra tene palmerias

Onde canta a Sabia

As aves que acqui gorgeiao

Nao gorgeiao como la.

"Nosso ceo teni mais estrellas

Nossos varzenes tem mais flores

Nossos bosques tem mais vida,

Nossos vida mais amores."

"Brava, little one," cried Uncle Prudente who had come out from his siesta refreshed and cool. "That was very prettily sung, little patriot. Have you children heard the news?"

"What news, my uncle?" asked Affonzo.

"That you are to go home with me to-morrow to see your grandmother."

"How glad I am!" cried Affonzo, and Lola danced up and down in delight, saying,

"It is long since we have been in Para, and the ride on the river will be so pleasant."

The next day was bright and fair and their sail down the great river as pleasant as they had anticipated. The air was cool and the sun partially under a cloud, so that the heat was not too great and the banks of the stream, with their trees and flowers, presented views as vivid and changing as a kaleidoscope.

The city of Para is one of the most important places in Brazil. From it are sent out into the world all the produce of the wonderful valley of the Amazon,—woods, rubber and fruits. Its markets are busy spots of industry, and its harbour teems with shipping.

The mother of the Senhor Dias lived in a handsome house on the edge of the town. Since the death of her husband she had lived with her only unmarried son, the Uncle Prudente of whom the children were so fond. She received the travellers warmly. Her son Martim's wife was very dear to her, his children her idols, especially Affonzo. He was his grandfather's image; with his flashing black eyes, his proud mouth, his quick, impetuous manner, he was so like the noble old man she had so loved, that he seemed to embody the youth of her beloved dead.

"You must remain for a long visit with me," she said to the children. "I have asked the children of friends to come and play with you in the garden this afternoon. Some of your school-mates will be here, Affonzo, and some little folk for Lola. I hope you will have a pleasant time."

"You are most kind, grandmamma," cried both children, and when their friends came, they all repaired to the shady garden behind the house.

There were about a dozen boys and girls all chattering at once, but in a moment's quiet Lola said,

"Let us play 'Dona Sancha.' I should like it so much and we have thirteen, just the right number."

"Yes," said a little girl named Catharina.

"There are seven girls and six boys. One of us must be it."

"Who shall be it?" they all cried merrily, and one of the larger girls stood them in a row and repeated,

"I am a little widow

From the seacoast there;

I wish to find a husband

But I can't tell where.

Shall I marry this one? Yes.

Shall I marry that one? No.

Shall I marry this one? Yes,

For I love him so."

The lot fell to a little black-eyed girl called Constancia, who was then blindfolded and around whom the others formed a circle by joining hands. Then all danced around Constancia singing,

"Madame Dona Sancha

Covered with silver and gold,

Take away your veil then,

Your eyes we would behold."

At this Constancia uncovered her face, and sang,

"I am the daughter of a count,

The grandchild of a king,

Behind a stone they made me hide,

A most peculiar thing."

Then the others sang,

"Valentin-tin-tin—

Who is married,

Who is married,

She who is not must remain alone."

At the last words the boys and girls let go of each other's hands and each one, including Constancia, made a rush for a partner. Lola was the one to be left out and she had to be blindfolded, and take Constancia's place in the centre of the ring. So the game went on, each girl taking her turn in the centre as often as she failed to catch a partner in the scramble.

When the children were tired of play, their grandmother sent out Christovao, an old white-haired negro who had once been a slave, and he showed them many wonderful tricks of juggling. He made flowers to bloom in their hats, money to grow on trees, and many other queer things to happen, and his pet monkey kept them laughing with his queer antics. Then they all sat down around the stone fountain and had a delicious luncheon of doces, cocada, and sweet cakes, and Affonzo and Lola went to bed that night quite delighted with their first day in Para.

CHAPTER VI

EN ROUTE TO RIO

PARA is one of the most beautiful of Brazilian cities, with large cool houses, and squares and gardens gay with wonderful orchids,—purple, crimson, gold and white.

The weeks spent at grandmamma's were full of delight to Affonzo and Lola, and they enjoyed all the pleasant happenings of life in the city. One day in October they sat in the garden playing with the pet monkey, a saucy little creature with a thousand cunning tricks and ways, almost human in his intelligence.

"I wonder how soon we shall go home," said Affonzo. "I begin to weary of doing nothing."

"I do not know," said Lola. "But I heard mamma say something strange about it to-day. She and my father were talking while I was playing with the cockatoo and mamma said, 'It will be a long trip and I should dislike to leave them behind.' 'It would do you little good to go with them,' said my father, and mamma replied that the worry of leaving them would take away all the pleasure of the trip if they were not to accompany her; then she saw me looking and bade my father be silent. What trip could they mean?"

"I am sure I do not know, and you should never remember a conversation not meant for you," said Affonzo, virtuously. Then, his curiosity getting the better of his virtue, "I wonder where they can be intending to go!"

"But if I should not remember what I hear, then you should not either," said Lola pertly, for she did not like to have Affonzo correct her.

"We are two quite different people," said Affonzo. "I am much older than you."

"When one is old, one should behave better than one who is young," Lola retorted.

"Both are quite old enough not to quarrel," said their mother's voice sternly, as she came up unnoticed. "What are you quarrelling about?"

Both children were silent and ashamed.

"If you dare not tell the cause, then cease the quarrel," said the Senhora. "And remember that well-bred children do not dispute. Now sit down while I tell you what is going to happen.

"Your father has intended for some time to make a business trip to Rio de Janeiro, going by boat from Para. He wishes me to go with him, for I have not been well of late, and he thought best to leave you two with your grandmother. I wished you to accompany me, and some news has just come which has caused him to give his consent.

"Your Uncle Juan, who went to study medicine in Philadelphia, married there a beautiful North American lady, and has a little daughter the age of Affonzo. She is named Maria and she had the great misfortune to lose her mother a few months ago. She grieves terribly and her father is bringing her to Brazil in the hope that among his people she will grow well and strong again. They will reach Rio de Janeiro in a short time, and we want to be there to see them. Would you like to go with us on this trip?"

"Indeed yes, mamma!" cried both in one breath. "When do we start?"

"To-morrow," she replied. "I did not tell you before, because I feared you would too much excite yourselves. Then too I thought something might happen to prevent our going and you would be disappointed."

"Hurrah," cried Affonzo. "We shall see Uncle Hilario!"

"And I shall see my cousin Martim!" cried Lola.

"Yes, we shall visit my dear brother, and you shall have a very happy time with two cousins to play with.

"Now you must be good children and give me a chance to pack up your clothes. No questions!" She held up her finger playfully. "Those you may save to ask me on ship-board. Here is a map which shows just where we are going, and you may trace out the course and Affonzo can tell you about all the places from his geography, Lola," and she left the two children poring over the geography, their tongues fairly clacking in their excitement.

The Icamiaba is a large steamer plying from Mañaos to Rio, and by noon the next day the little party of four were safely embarked and the steamer made its way out of the beautiful harbour. The long voyage was begun, but to Affonzo and Lola it was not tedious, for, the only children on board, they soon became pets with all and were in a fair way to being spoiled with attention. The second day out the steamer made its first stop at Pernambuco on the easternmost point of Brazil, and the children watched the entrance into the harbour with great interest.

"Pernambuco is called the Venice of America," said their father. "You know Venice is an Italian city built on islands, with waterways instead of streets, and here there are so many canals and arms of water reaching in from the sea that Pernambuco is called the Venice of America."

"What a lot of steamers there are!" exclaimed Affonzo as they approached the reef which protects the harbour. This reef runs along the Brazilian coast for hundreds of miles, forming a natural breakwater, sometimes twelve feet above high tide.

"N-I-L-E," spelled Affonzo as they passed a huge steamer anchored outside the harbour. "What kind of a boat is that?"

"English," said his father. "The English run a line of steamers from Southampton to Lisbon, and thence to Rio Janeiro. These boats carry a thousand passengers, and are so large that they cannot go through the cut in the breakwater."

"Oh, papa! What a queer building! What is it?" asked Lola, as they passed an odd-looking fort on the rocks.

"That is a relic of Dutch days in Brazil," said the Senhor. "You know the Dutch once laid claim to all this part of the country."

"Did they?" asked Lola in surprise. "How did they get here and what became of them?"

"It is a long story, little one, but quite an interesting one," said her father. "You know Brazil was discovered by a Portuguese, Pedro Alvarez Cabral, who sailed into the Bay of Porto Seguro at Bahia, April 25, 1500, and took possession of the land in the name of the Portuguese crown, naming it Vera

Cruz. The Spaniards had made discoveries in the north of South America, the English and French hadcome in along the Amazon and within the next few years the Dutch entered the river and built forts on the Xingu. Then came a long struggle between the Dutch and the Portuguese as to who should possess the land. In 1624, a Dutch admiral took possession of Bahia, but a handful of Portuguese recaptured the place the next year; then came a succession of battles, first the Dutch being victorious, then the Portuguese. At last the Dutch sent Prince Maurice of Nassau as Governor General of their possessions in Brazil, but he returned to Holland in 1644 and from that time on the Portuguese were successful. They laid siege to Pernambuco (then called Recife) and blockaded the port with sea forces while the land army assaulted it on the other side. The Dutch surrendered in 1654 and Brazil became a Portuguese colony."

"Then I suppose everything was peaceful," said Affonzo, but his father laughed and said,

"There has not been much peace in Brazil since the Portuguese first discovered it. After the foreigners left, the Indians remained unconquered, and the Portuguese sent many expeditions against the natives in the interior. Many adventurers went on these expeditions, and they were called Bandierantes. They treated the Indians cruelly and enslaved many, although the Pope had forbidden making slaves of the Indians.

"Another fight which took place near here was with negro slaves. Some of them escaped and fled to the forest of Palmeiras, in the Province of Alagoas. Here they maintained a colony for sixty years and were only subdued in 1697. Some of their chiefs leaped from a high rock into the sea rather than be captured."

"How did they get slaves in our country?" asked Lola.

"That's a rather big subject for such a little girl," said her father. "The early settlers could not get any one to work for them, so they brought black people from Africa, as did most of the Southern countries. One good thing was that here slavery was abolished without a drop of blood being shed, while in North America they had a terrible war.

"Now we are entering the harbour, Affonzo. See how many ships! In one year there were one thousand one hundred and eighty-one ships here! They come from all parts of the world, laden with all manner of things, but they nearly all go away freighted with sugar. There are thousands of tons of it exported every year. The boat will stop here some hours, so we will go ashore and drive about the city."

"Oh, thank you, papa," cried the children, and their mother added, "It will be a pleasant change from the ship."

So the four went ashore and drove about the cheerful city, with its gaily painted houses, passing one public building glazed in yellow and green tiles, another in imitation pink marble trimmed in sky blue. Crossing a long bridge, they saw magnificent gardens with brilliant flowering plants, and the fine fruit-market where they purchased the luscious Pernambuco abacoxi the finest-flavoured pineapple in the world.

"It is a very fine city," said Affonzo as they returned to the steamer.

"But not as handsome as Para," said Lola. "That's the prettiest city in all Brazil," and her father laughed.

When they steamed into Bahia two days later just at twilight, she still insisted that Para was the most beautiful place in the world, but Affonzo was delighted with Bahia.

"Capt. Diego Alvarez was one of the early explorers here," said the Senhor, as they sat upon the deck in the moonlight, watching the crescent of lights which rise from the harbour toward heaven, for the main portion of Bahia is built upon a high bluff overlooking the river.

"He was captured by the Indians and was about to be killed, when the chief's daughter threw herself in front of him and saved his life. Alvarez fell in love with her and married her, taking her with him to France, where she was honoured and cared for all her life. Some of the best families in Bahia boast that she is their ancestor."

"What are sent out from here?" asked Affonzo.

"Thousands and thousands of cocoanuts, for one thing," said the Senhor. "It is a fortune for a family to have a cocoa plantation, for the trees produce from fifty to eighty years, and need little attention after the first year or two. They are very easy to raise. After planting, the weeds are kept away from the trees, and during the first year, banana plants are grown between the rows to shade the young trees. The fourth year the first crop is gathered and the trees produce two hundred clusters of fruit with thirty or forty nuts each. People net about sixty thousand dollars a year from a plantation of fifty thousand trees."

"It must pay to raise cocoanuts at that rate," said Affonzo. "Does manaioca pay as well?"

"Not quite, but it is about as easy to raise. Everyone has to have manaioca. The rich use if for puddings and desserts in the form of tapioca, while the poor people use the fariulia de manaioca as their chief food. It also makes good starch, for the roots ground up in water deposit their starch as a fine white powder.

"A farm of twelve acres belonging to a friend of mine and planted with forty thousand plants produces eighty thousand pounds of tapioca, which at the lowest price brings two thousand four hundred and twenty-five dollars."

"The children are growing to be regular little encyclopedias," said the Senhora. "They must go to bed now, or I am afraid their brains will burst with so much knowledge."

"Not much danger of that," laughed the Senhor. "Most of it goes in at one ear and comes out the other," but Lola and Affonzo exclaimed indignantly, "Oh, no, papa, indeed it does not."

CHAPTER VII
IN THE CAPITAL

A WEEK after they had left home, the children saw for the first time the harbour of Rio de Janeiro, the Icamiaba entering the beautiful bay between the Sugar Loaf Mountain and the Fortress of Santa Cruz, in all the glory of a Brazilian sunset.

At the left was the curious mountain called Seria dos Orgaos, so named from its resemblance to a church organ. Charming islets dotted the bay, and orange trees, bananas, always green and loaded with fruit, and flowers everywhere met the eye.

Mountains seemed to rise from the sea; the cliffs are nearly perpendicular with scarce a yard of greensward at the water's edge, and they guard jealously the most beautiful harbour in the world. Scarcely two ships can enter between the islands marking the entrance of the bay, which is so narrow that the discoverer thought it a river and named it "Rio." Within, however, the sheet of water widens until it is a glorious inner sea, called by the Indians, "Nictheroy"—Hidden Waters.

The houses of the city, walled in stucco, are of a deep canary yellow with roofs tiled in deep red, turning to fire beneath the sun's departing rays.

"How beautiful it is," said the Senhora. "It seems to me my old home never looked so fair!"

"It is one of the most beautiful places in the world," said her husband. "See those large buildings, children. That is the Sailors' Hospital on Ilha da Governador, which was once used as a hunting preserve by the royal family. It is a beautiful island and many strange things have happened there. One was the death of the founder of the city, Estacio de Sa. He was a famous Indian fighter, and here received a fatal wound from an arrow."

"Something seems to have happened everywhere in Brazil," said Lola. "How near we are to land."

"Yes," cried her mother. "And there is your uncle waving his hat upon the wharf. Martim is with him! He sees us! Wave to him, daughter!" and the usually calm Senhora, flushed and excited, waved her handkerchief, smiling happily.

"I have not seen you look so gay for many months," said her husband, and she replied, "It is so long since I have seen my dear old home and my own people!"

Soon the ship was made fast, and the children stepped off the gang plank to be greeted warmly by the uncle whom they had not seen since Lola was a baby, and the cousin whom they had never seen before.

"Your Aunt Luiza and Maria are anxiously awaiting you at home," he said. "Here is the carriage, so we will hasten."

"Drive through the Street do Ouvidor, papa, will you not?" asked Martim. "It is so gay with the French shops, my cousins will enjoy it."

Martim was a handsome boy of twelve, with a bright, pleasant face, an only child, for the Senhor and Senhora Lopez had lost all their other children in an epidemic of yellow fever some years before.

"What are those men doing with long poles over their shoulders," asked Lola, pointing to several men who carried bamboo rods with baskets hung at the ends.

"They are fish and vegetable vendors," Martim replied. "Some of those baskets weigh over a hundred pounds. Those other men withthe gaily-painted tin trunks on their backs peddle clothing."

"They make a lot of noise," said Affonzo.

"Yes, they warn people they are coming by clapping together two pieces of wood fastened to their hands by a leather strap," said his cousin.

"Oh! What a beautiful statue!" cried Lola.

"That is the Emperor Dom Pedro I," said her uncle. "It was made by a noted French sculptor and represents the Emperor shouting the Brazilian watch word 'Independencia ou morte.' Here we are at home!" as the carriage turned into a broad street on either side of which were old fashioned houses with broad verandas and red and white blinds. "There is Aunt Luiza waiting to welcome you!"

The children jumped out of the carriage and ran to meet their aunt, who kissed them warmly and drew forward a tall girl of ten, who looked pale and sad. Her hair was very light, her eyes deep blue, and she was a great contrast to black-eyed, brown-cheeked Lola.

"This is Maria, your North American cousin," said their aunt, and Lola kissed her warmly on either cheek.

"We are so glad to have you come," she said. "And my mother is going to take you home with us for a nice long visit. I have always wanted a sister, so let us play we are sisters."

Maria kissed her and smiled, while Aunt Luiza said, "Come, children, it is very late; dinner is waiting and then all you little folk must get to bed early so you will be ready for to-morrow. There are ever so many things for you to see."

Early next day the four cousins set out for a morning's sight-seeing, accompanied by their Uncle Hilario. The Senhor Lopez was one of those rare men who are really fond of children, and he enjoyed their society.

Most of the streets of the city have no curbing, and the children had to be careful lest they be run down by passing carriages.

Their uncle decided first to take them to the famous Botanical Gardens and as they entered the main gateway, they saw the avenue of fine royal palms.

"The avenue is almost half a mile long," said the Senhor. "And the trees are a hundred feet high."

"Aren't they fine," said Affonzo. "They are the tallest palms I ever saw."

"They meet together at the top and form a regular archway the whole length of the walk," said Martim.

"What is that very high mountain?" asked Lola.

"That is the Corcovado, and some day we shall go over there and ascend it," said Martim. "We shall have to start very early in the morning, for it is a long trip."

"Here comes Doctor Barbosa, papa," said Martim. "I wonder if he will go around the gardens with us."

"Perhaps he will, if he is not too busy. If he does, he can tell you all about the trees and flowers for he has explored the country along the Amazon and knows all about the Brazilian flora."

As the Senhor spoke, Doctor Barbosa came up smiling, for he and Senhor Lopez were old friends.

"You have quite a bevy of little folk with you to-day," he said pleasantly.

"This is my nephew, Affonzo Diaz, Doctor Barbosa," said the Senhor. "And these girls are my nieces, Charlotta and Maria. Of course you know Martim."

"I am very glad to see you all," said the doctor with a smile.

"This is the first visit of Affonzo and his sister to our city," said Senhor Lopez.

"Indeed," replied the doctor. "I really think then that you should let me help show them around the gardens. I have a few moments of leisure just now, that I will be glad to devote to you."

"That will be delightful," said the Senhor. "You know so much about this place and I so little that I am sure the children will much prefer you as a guide." Bowing in appreciation of the compliment, the doctor led the party down the avenue.

"These gardens," he said, pointing down across the avenue, "as you see, are on the border of a large sheet of water. That is called the Lagoa de Rodrigo Freitas, and is separated from the sea only by a narrow strip of sand."

"What are those crooked, twisted trees," asked Lola, as they passed into another long avenue.

"They are mangoes. They are not very handsome to look at, but you know what delicious fruit they bear."

"Indeed I do," said Lola.

"This," said the doctor, pointing to a tall palm beside the pathway, "is a Bahia palm. It is from trees of this kind that your brooms and brushes at home are made."

Next they saw the great candelabra tree.

"It looks," said Maria, "as if it were already to be lighted for church, doesn't it?"

"See the beautiful grove of orange trees," said the Senhor.

"Oh yes," said Affonzo. "And the trees have both fruit and blossoms on them."

"That is not at all uncommon with many of our tropical fruit trees," said Doctor Barbosa.

"Many of the trees here," he continued, "are useful for other purposes than fruit-bearing. There is the cow tree over yonder. Its sap looks like milk, and when exposed to the air is soon changed to glue, and from this a useful cement is made."

As the party approached a little lake in the centre of the gardens, they saw a small eight-sided pavilion. On its top was a bust.

"Whose statue is that?" asked Affonzo.

"If you will step closer, you can read the inscription on the tablet," said the doctor. "And that will answer your question."

"To the Memory of Friar Leandro do Sacramento of the Order of Carmelites, a graduate in the natural sciences at the University of Coimbra, first professor of botany in the School of Medicine in Rio, and first technical director of the Botanical Gardens."

"If I can do as much for this beautiful park as Friar Leandro did, I shall be content," said Doctor Barbosa.

"What a magnificent palm that is!" said the Senhor Lopez, as they turned from the pavilion and came in sight of an unusually tall tree.

"Yes," said the doctor, "that is a royal palm, over one hundred and twenty-five feet high. The seed is said to have been brought here by a Portuguese naval officer who escaped from prison on the Isle de France. It was planted with great care by the regent, Dom Joao himself, and here is the splendid result. I am sorry that I must leave you now, but you must come again to see the gardens."

"Thank you very much for all that you have shown us," said Affonzo, and all the children chorused, "Thank you very much."

"It is past noon and we ought to be at home now," said the Senhor looking at his watch.

"I believe I am hungry," said Martim, "though I hadn't thought about it before."

So they all went back to the house with appetites such as the balmy air of Rio gives to young and vigorous boys and girls.

CHAPTER VIII

A GALA DAY IN RIO

IN the fortnight which followed the four cousins became very well acquainted with each other. Maria soon lost her shyness, and taught the others many new games and sports, while they in turn taught her the Brazilian ones which her father had played when a boy at home.

The little Brazilians found their North American cousin very interesting. She was different from them in many ways and they never tired of hearing her tell of things in the United States. Although admiring her father's country very much, she was devoted to her mother's as well, and could never be made to admit that things were better in South America than they were in the north.

"Come, children," said the Senhora Lopez one morning, "this is the day of the inauguration. The President himself has given your father tickets, for they are great friends and we must all be ready early so as to escape the crowd."

"Indeed, mamma," said Martim, "I think the crowd's the greatest fun of all. I shall never forget the procession the day of the parade in honour of your Senhor Root, Maria. It was one of the finest we ever had in Rio."

"I wish I had seen it," said Maria. "When our President is inaugurated we have grand processions in Washington. My grandfather took me to the last one, and it was splendid."

"Our inauguration procession is fine, too. You will see to-day that they know how to do things down here as well as you do," said Martim, as they started for the reviewing-stand.

"I don't doubt that," said Maria pleasantly. "But I can't quite make out why you have a President at all. Brazil used to be an empire and have a splendid emperor. You showed me his statue in the park. What became of him?"

"The last emperor of Brazil is dead, my child," said her uncle. "He died in Paris in 1891, some said of a broken heart, because he had been sent away from his beloved Brazil."

"Why did you send him away; wasn't he a good man?" asked Maria.

"Yes, indeed, very good, and many of the people were very fond of him," was the reply. "He was always interested in the people and tried to arrange the laws for their best interests. He was very democratic and travelled about a great deal, keeping his eyes wide open to learn everything which might help his people. He even went to your United States at the time of the Centennial in Philadelphia."

"If he was so good, why did they send him away?" asked Maria puzzled.

"It is rather hard to explain politics to little folk," said her uncle, smiling.

"Some of the Brazilians wanted to have a republic like the United States, for they thought that country was so prosperous that they wanted Brazil to be like it.

"The people thought that the United States had progressed more rapidly and was more prosperous than Brazil and they did not see why their own land should not be as great or greater than any other American country. Brazil was the only South American country which was not a republic. I think the chief reason, however, was that the heir to the throne was not at all liked, and the Brazilians were afraid that he would not be as wise a ruler as Dom Pedro had been. Even those who most wanted a republic were sorry to have the old emperor expelled, and many of them cried bitterly when he went away."

"I should think they might have waited until he died," said Maria. "If he was old he wouldn't have lived long, and then they needn't have had his heir whom they didn't like. I do not think it was nice at all to send him away when he had always been good and kind."

"If it had been in the United States you would have shot him, like you do your Presidents, wouldn't you?" asked Affonzo mischievously, for he loved to tease his cousin.

"We have only had three Presidents killed out of twenty-six," said Maria. "How many of yours have been assassinated?"

"I'm sure I don't know," said Affonzo, rather taken aback at the quickness of her retort.

"In the early days," said Uncle Hilario, "before the republic was very firmly established, the Presidents used to have to be taken from the army so they could fight to keep their positions. Now, however, things are quieter and we do not have to have our ruler backed by sword and guns."

"Here we are at the grand stand. The music is just beginning to draw near. Hurrah! There come the soldiers!" cried Affonzo. "Aren't they fine-looking fellows!"

"What gorgeous uniforms they have!" cried Lola, and Maria exclaimed,

"Aren't the plumed horses splendid!" And they chattered all at once till their uncle fairly covered his ears with his hands.

They had a good look at the two Presidents—President Campos-Salles whose term of office was just over, and Affonzo Penna who was the new President—and returned home quite excited with the events of the morning.

Next day they had planned an excursion to the top of Corcovado, that beautiful mountain which rises above Rio, serene and lofty, toward the clouds, and all was excitement as the little party started off.

"Think of having mamma with us!" cried Lola. "Uncle Hilario, have you and mamma been up the mountain before?"

"I should say we had," he laughed, then turning to his sister, "Do you remember the time we were caught in the terrible storm?"

"It was a terrific cloud burst, but we didn't mind it," she said, laughing too. "In those days climbing Corcovado was something of a feat. There was no cog-wheel railway as there is to-day but only a bridle-path. We had to start long before daybreak and climb up the side of the mountain. We had to take servants along to carry provisions and there was always a large party going.

"The time your uncle speaks of, he and I got separated from the rest of the party going down and we came near losing our way entirely. There came up a terrible storm and when we finally arrived at home an hour after the others we were drenched to the skin, and they had sent people out to hunt for us.

"It is a very different thing to-day to go up the mountain seated in a carriage, find a café at the top, and have nothing to do but look at the sights as we pass. They are well worth looking at! See! There is the bay, its water as blue as the sky, and you get a fine view of the old aqueduct."

"I wondered what that was," said Maria. "It looks like the pictures I have seen of the Campagna at Rome. Is it made of stone?"

"Yes," said her uncle. "It was built of stone nearly two hundred years ago and is over four miles long. In some places its arches are over sixty feet high and it is as strong as when it was built. Through it passes all the water drunk in Rio, and is so delicious that we have a saying 'Who has drunk of the waters of Carioca can drink no other water,' and 'When you have drunk of the water of Carioca, you can live nowhere else but here.'"

"When Rio people speak of the friends who have lived in Rio they say, 'He is a Cariocan.'"

"Then mamma is a Cariocan!" cried Lola, and Maria added,

"And my father, too."

"It seems to almost walk across the chasm," said Affonzo. "Where does the water come from?"

"When we reach the top of the mountain, I will show you," said his uncle. "See those magnificent waterfalls and cascades! The scenery around here is as fine as any in Brazil."

"It is almost as nice as the White Mountains at home," said Maria wickedly. She loved to stir up her cousins and knew that to compare anything with the States always provoked a discussion. This time her remarks were met with a storm of protest, at which she only laughed naughtily.

"I don't believe you have such trees," said Lola at last. "There are mangoes, tamarinds, bread-fruits, bananas, cocoa trees, oranges and palms all growing together. Aren't they splendid?"

"Yes, indeed," said Maria. "And the flowers are simply gorgeous. Those trees with the flowering vine all draped around them and hanging down in long racemes are as beautiful as anything I ever saw."

"Here we are at the end of the railway," said Martim. "Now for a climb."

It was but a short distance to the top, and the children hurried along, followed more slowly by their elders.

"Here we are at last," said the Senhor as they reached the top. "Now you can see seventy miles, for there is Organ Mount fifty miles away, and yonder is Cape Frio, which is seventy miles away."

"Among the mountain peaks there lies the sea of gold," said Uncle Hilario. "There is a tale told that in the early Portuguese days inBrazil a murderer, who had been condemned to death, escaped from prison and fled to the hills. He wandered about, fed only by the bounty of the forest and at last he discovered the Lake of Gold. From its shining sands he made a fortune, and returned in two years to Rio to buy his pardon."

"The Lake of Gold," said Affonzo. "I wonder if that is where the Gilded Man washed himself."

"Who was the Gilded Man?" asked Maria.

"It's an Indian story Vicente told me," said Affonzo.

"Do tell it to me," she said, and he told her the quaint tale with which she was delighted.

They lunched in picnic fashion on the grass and had a merry time, resting afterwards while the Senhora and Uncle Hilario told them stories of old days in Brazil. At last it came time to return and the two boys, after whispering together went to their uncle with a request.

"May we not walk down?" Martim asked. "We won't get lost and we want to do what you and mother did."

"Oh, do let us!" cried Maria, who always wanted to do every thing the boys did, but the Senhora shook her head. At last it was arranged that Uncle Hilario should walk down with the boys, while the girls went discreetly home in the train with the Senhora. The boys were jubilant.

"See the ships, uncle," cried Affonzo as they looked across the bay to the broad Atlantic. "They are just over the horizon line. What's that puff of smoke for?" as a puff came from a ship nearing the harbour.

"Watch the fort," said the Senhor, and there another puff was seen. "Eyes are better than ears at this range. That was a salute from the ship answered by the guns from the fort. We can see the smoke, but cannot hear the report.

"Here is the source of Carioca. The name is from an Indian word, Kaa-ry-og, and means 'the house of the streams from the woods.' See how the stream is shaded by these giant trees? That is what makes it so cold. The water flows amidst all manner of sweet-smelling aromatic plants, and goes into an aqueduct full of pleasant scents. It is said to have some medicinal qualities."

"It is nice enough here to cure any sickness," said Martim, and they went slowly on down the mountain, following the same bridle-path which their uncle had followed so many years before, reaching home without any accident, tired but delighted with the tramp.

CHAPTER IX

THE COFFEE PLANTATION

THE Senhor Lopez' business was to export coffee, as that of his brother-in-law was to export rubber. He had a large coffee fazenda in Sao Paulo, the province of Brazil most devoted to coffee raising, and he often went there to inspect the plantation. He suggested therefore that his wife, his sister, and the children should spend a week with him at the fazenda, and the two mothers decided to do so, knowing how much pleasure it would give the little folk. It was an all day's ride to Sao Paulo, but there was so much to see as the train moved over the plains, across rivers and through forests and hills, that the children did not find it tiresome, and were very bright and gay as, just at sunset, they neared Sao Paulo.

"This is one of the finest cities of Brazil," said their uncle. "Ten years ago it was not a large place but now it has three hundred thousand people, many beautiful buildings, electric lights and trolley cars. It has also some very good schools and colleges, and students come here from all parts of the country. Perhaps Affonzo will go to college here some day."

"It seems a good ways from home," said the boy. "But uncle," he added, as they passed a crowd of queer looking people in the station, "what a lot of foreigners there are here!"

"Yes, more than in any other Brazilian city. A number of Italians work in the mills and on the farms, and the Germans are on the coffee plantations.

"To-night we will rest, and to-morrow morning we will see Sao Paulo, and in the afternoon go to the fazenda," said the Senhor, as they reached the hotel.

The next day they had a pleasant drive through the city and saw many interesting things.

"Mackenzie College is one of the best seats of learning in Brazil," said the uncle. "It is on the plan of the North American colleges, with kindergarten, primary grades and grammar school. There is also a normal school and a manual training shop."

"You see, you have to copy us," said Maria with a laugh. "All the schools in the States are good. You ought to live there."

Martim made a wry face.

"Maybe they are," he said, "but I don't believe I'd care to live in the States just on account of the schools when I can live here, and have a school just as good."

"Children!" said Martim's mother, but his father hastily interposed,

"Mackenzie College is named for Mr. John G. Mackenzie, of New York City, who gave a large sum of money to build it. But here we are at the Garden of Light. Now you may get out of the carriage and rest yourselves by running about these magnificent alleys of trees, seeing the lakes and fountains."

"Maria and Martim do not get along as well as the little girl and Affonzo," he said to his wife, as soon as the children were out of sight.

"It doesn't matter," she said serenely. "It does not hurt either of them to argue if it doesn't go too far. Children are far better for not being noticed. Affonzo gets along better with his cousin because he has Lola to quarrel with; Martim grows selfish from being too much alone." She sighed and her husband's face clouded as he thought of the children they had lost.

"We will keep Maria with us if the father is willing, as long as she is in Brazil."

"Better still, let both Maria and Martim return home with us," said the Senhora Dias. "Then all four young folk will learn to accommodate themselves to each other."

"That is an excellent plan, and it is kind in you to suggest it," said the Senhora Lopez, and her husband added,

"We shall try to arrange it that way."

"Come, children," he called a few minutes later. "We must return for lunch now as we drive to the fazenda afterwards. Do you know what we old folk have been planning?"

"No, papa, what is it?" asked Martim.

"Something pleasant, I am sure," said Lola. "For you are the dearest uncle in the world."

"Thank you, little flatterer," he pinched her cheek playfully. "It is that you four cousins are all to return to Para for the winter."

"Oh, delightful," cried Lola.

"How nice!" Maria said, and the boys seemed equally pleased.

The afternoon air was clear and bracing, and the children were in high spirits as the party drove to the fazenda.

The road wound through a beautiful country, past vineyards, and tea and coffee plantations, for Sao Paulo is one of the most productive provinces of Brazil. As they passed row after row of small trees Lola said,

"What pretty, glossy leaves those trees have!"

"Those are coffee trees," said Martim. "They grow about twelve feet tall."

"But where are the brown berries," asked Maria. "Are they all picked?"

Martim laughed.

"It's easy to see that you've never seen coffee growing," he said. "Did you think you could go and pick the browned berries and stew a pot of coffee?"

"No," said Maria demurely, "because we don't 'stew' coffee where I live."

Everybody laughed at this passage-at-arms between the two children, and Senhor Lopez said,

"We are beginning to see trees belonging to our plantation now. It is three miles square and we have just reached the edge of the land. The house is still three miles away."

"How does the coffee grow, Uncle Hilario?" asked Maria.

"Do you see the cluster of green pods on the trees, my dear? Well, seeds are within the pods, and when they are ripened must be dried, roasted and ground before they are ready for your coffee-pot. Later in the season the fruit turns bright red in colour, and makes a vivid contrast to the foliage of the trees, which is green the year around."

"Are the trees planted, or do they grow wild like our rubber trees?" asked Affonzo.

"They are planted in rows and sometimes grow as high as twenty-five feet. Usually they are between ten and fifteen feet high when they first bear fruit," said the Senhor. "It takes from three to five years for them to bear."

"When is the harvest time?" asked Maria.

"We have two crops so there are two harvests, one in February and one in August. Sometimes you see fruit and flowers on the same tree at the same time. The blossoms grow in little white bunches and are very fragrant."

"I should think it would take a lot of people to pick all this coffee," said Affonzo.

"It does. If you were to be here next February you would see hundreds of negroes and Italians, men, women, and children, busy up and down these long rows. Many of them live in those little houses," he said, pointing to a street lined with small wooden huts crowded close together. About the houses were scores of small, dark-skinned children at play.

"At the present time," said the Senhor, "the men and women are at work in the sheds and ware-houses making the coffee ready for market. We shall ship thousands of pounds next month. To-morrow I will take you about and show you what we have to do. I wish you might have been here during the harvest season. It is very interesting to watch the pickers with the huge baskets strapped to their shoulders. There is great rivalry among them to see who can be the fastest picker on the place."

Before they reached the fazenda their carriage passed through two gates which closed after them with a spring, and the Senhor said,

"The fazenda factory is always enclosed by one and sometimes two fences, for the cattle graze loose with only a pickaninny or themadrinla to watch them."

"It looks like a fortress," said Maria.

"Yes, and some fazendas are called 'fortaleza' for that very reason," said her uncle.

"It is really very much like the old fortresses of feudal times, within the walls of which went on all manner of things. Inside the fazenda palisades there are the houses of the labourers, apothecary's shop, hospital, warehouses, and terrerios, besides the house of the owner."

"Why are there so few trees?" asked Lola.

"Nearly all the trees are cut down to make pasture lands and only a few shade trees are left, such as those fine palms. Here we are at the house. When you are rested I will take you about and show you how the coffee is made ready for market."

CHAPTER X
A TREAT IN PROSPECT

THE week at the fazenda was a time of pleasant rest to the elders and full of delight to the children. They rode the horses and saw the cows milked and fed the pigs. These last were always taken very good care of by the fazendeiro, for they afford the principal food for all on the plantation.

There was very little in regard to coffee-raising that the children did not learn, for their inquisitive little noses were poked into every shed and room to see what was going on. Their Uncle Hilario went with them one day and explained it all fully while they listened eagerly.

"First the coffee goes to this large shed and is dumped into the great vat," he said. "The iron thing in the centre of the vat is the pulping machine. You see it is round like a cylinder and covered with teeth, and there are holes in the bottom. The teeth are covered on one side with a curved sheet of metal. When the cylinder revolves, water is turned into the vat, and as it flows through, the seeds are carried through the holes in the cylinder into tanks where the remaining matter is washed away.

"Then they go to the drying terrace," he said as they left the building and went toward a large piece of ground exposed to the blazing sun and covered with cement. "Here it is. After the pulp has been removed from the seeds there is left a thin skin. The seeds are spread in thin layers upon the ground and left to dry thoroughly in the sun, while workmen constantly turn them over and over with rakes to hasten the drying."

"How long does it take to dry them?" asked Martim.

"Several weeks," said his father. "On some fazendas they use steam heat, but we like the sun-dried coffee much the best. After the seeds are thoroughly dried they are taken to another building and passed through heavy rollers and the chaff separated and blown away.

"Now we will go to the sorting room," and they entered a long, low building where a number of women and girls were working at long tables piled with heaps of coffee berries. Men were constantly bringing in baskets full of the berries, which the women and girls sorted into different grades according to their quality.

"How fast their fingers fly," said Maria. "I don't see how they do it."

"They have done it so often and practice makes perfect," said her uncle. "As they sort the seeds they put them in sacks and the men carry them to another ware-house, where they are packed in sacks and weighed ready to be shipped."

"Uncle, what are those girls doing who are flying about everywhere with sieves in their hands?" asked Lola.

"They gather up all the berries which the men scatter as they carry the coffee about," he answered. "You see we do not want to waste anything.

"Do you see those wagons being loaded? The coffee in those sacks is ready to go to Sao Paulo, and thence to Santos to be shipped to North America. Our coffee goes to every part of the world, for the coffee of the Fazenda Esperança is considered especially good.

"Now you have followed the coffee berry from the tree to the market and I hope you will try to remember all about it, for the coffee industry is one of the greatest in the country."

"It's ever so interesting, uncle," said Maria. "And thank you for telling us about it."

"I have enjoyed it more than you have," he answered. "It is a pleasure to talk to such eager little listeners.

"Rest yourselves now, for you must be tired with all this tramping. I am going to the house to see your mother about some plans for to-morrow."

"Do tell us, uncle," they all cried, but he only shook his head and laughed as he went away.

"I shall simply die of curiosity if I do not find out what uncle is planning," said Maria.

"I don't see what good that would do," said Martim, "for you wouldn't be likely to either know about it or to do it if you were dead."

Maria made a naughty little face at him, and a quarrel seemed imminent when Lola, who had gone to the house when her uncle did, came running toward them waving her hand wildly.

"Oh! What do you think!" she cried as she ran up to them. "The loveliest thing has happened."

"What?" cried all the children at once, but Lola was too out of breath to answer.

"Uncle Hilario is certainly a darling!" she said at last. "He has prepared the loveliest treat for us! He says that to-morrow we all start for the Falls of Iguazu, and Maria, your father has come and—" but she had no chance to finish her sentence, for Martim shouted, "The Falls of Iguazu! Hurrah!" and ran off to the house, while Maria with a squeal of "Daddy!" pelted after him as fast as she could go. Lola and Affonzo looked at each other and laughed.

"What's it all about, Lolita?" he asked and she answered,

"Uncle Hilario told me that they had only been awaiting Uncle Juan's arrival to make the excursion to these wonderful falls and that we start to-morrow."

"Where are the falls?" asked Affonzo.

"Indeed, I don't know, but it is several days' journey and we can go only part of the way by train. We must take a boat and perhaps ride upon burros. It is far in the woods, and very few people go there."

"Let us go and find out all about it," said Affonzo, and the two children hurried to the house as the rest of the party had done.

There they found considerable excitement, every one asking a thousand questions which were not answered until the mothers placed their fingers in their ears and demanded silence. Maria was seated upon her father's knees, her usually sober little face bright with happiness, as she whispered to Lola, "He is going to Para with us, to stay all winter, so I can be with him and have you too!" Lola gave her hand a loving squeeze, but said nothing, for Uncle Hilario began to speak.

"The Falls of Iguazu, children, are one of the most beautiful places in all Brazil. They lie at the joining of the Parana and Iguazurivers, at the point where the frontiers of Brazil, Paraguay and Argentina meet. We will go by rail to Curitaba but part of the way lies through the mountains and will be hard to travel. The sail down the river will be delightful. Your mother, Martim, will stay here on the plantation, and any one who wishes may stay with her. Uncle Juan, Martim and I, your father and mother, Lola, are going. Who else wants to be in the party?"

"I!" cried all three children at once, and Lola added,

"We'll be so good, uncle, if we can only go!"

"Well, you may all go, then," said the Senhor Lopez, "and I think it will be a delightful trip. No—" as they all started to ask questions—"don't ask me a thing to-day. There will be plenty of time to talk about it on our journey, and I have not a moment to spare, for it takes a great deal of planning to get such a party off."

"Yes, and I have all I can possibly attend to," said Lola's mother. "So you little folk must amuse yourselves."

"I am the only one who has nothing to do," said Uncle Juan. "Suppose you all come out under the palms with me, and I will try to tell you something of the country we are going to see." So joyfully they trooped after him and listened spellbound to his words.

"The country where we are going," he said, "is called the 'Land of the Missiones' because it is here that the early missions were founded by the Jesuits. These devoted men went all over that part of Brazil trying to convert the Indians and making settlements, some of which are still standing after two hundred years. San Ignacio, though deserted by the Indians, is still in existence near Iguazu and there was once there a prosperous Indian settlement built around a plaza, with a school, dwelling houses and a church.

"The falls are magnificent, but you will have to wait and see them before you can understand how really beautiful they are."

"Not so beautiful as Niagara, father, of course!" said Maria, and her father said, "Some people think they are quite as fine, daughter; but have you a chip on your shoulder now about the States? Maria would never admit to any North American that anything in the States could be finer than it was down here," he added to the boys.

Martim exclaimed, "Well, she's a queer sort of a girl! She never would let us praise anything here, because she'd always say the States were finer."

"The States were mamma's," she murmured, and her father held her close and kissed her as he whispered, "Little Loyalty!"

CHAPTER XI
THE FALLS OF IGUAZU

THE morning dawned cool and pleasant. All were ready for an early start and there followed a week of delight for the children. The railway journey over, they took their way through the forests, over plains and across rivers. In some the hoofs of the horses or of the sure-footed little burros the children rode sank in the sand which covered the land as at one time the sea had covered it. Again, trees appeared, and at last they reached the virgin forest where monkeys scampered among the trees and the cries of parrots were heard in the air, as their brilliant plumage flashed in the sunlight.

At times the bridle path was so narrow that no two horses could have passed each other had they met.

Convolvulus and creeping plants encircled the huge trees, and, swaying in the breeze, long vines swung gracefully down, often forming natural swings in which the children delighted. At night the party camped in tents, the negro servants cooking wonderful meals from the game shot during the day.

The days were not too hot and at night a fire was often necessary, for when the terral did not blow from the land the veracaowafted zephyrs from the ocean. The air was laden with the subtle perfume of the magnolia and orange blossom, and life seemed an existence of pleasure and joy.

The Senhor's trip had not been all for pleasure. It was his intention to increase his export trade in native woods, and he had made the journey through the forest to see whether it would be possible to get wood to the sea, were he to buy a tract of land in this region. The children, however, knew nothing about this. They were occupied with having a good time, and they were having it.

Martim and Affonzo hunted and fished, while the girls vied with each other in weaving rush baskets and in making flower-chains of the wonderful flowers which grew everywhere along the road, in gorgeous beauty.

As they neared Iguazu, the roar of the cataract could be heard for miles, and when they finally saw the falls, beyond the first surprised "Oh!" which broke from all, there was nothing said.

The river Iguazu makes a sharp bend above the falls and a portion of it rushes around the inner bank and falls into a gorge two hundred and ten feet deep; the remainder of the current, however, sweeps over the edge of a cliff and making two great leaps of a hundred feet falls in a huge half moon three thousand feet wide. All about was the most charming Brazilian scenery, with trees over one hundred feet high overgrown with tropical vines, and above all shone the deep blue of the tropical sky.

"Well, little Yankee, how about Niagara now?" asked Martim teasingly.

"There's only one Niagara," said Maria sturdily, and her father added,

"Niagara and Iguazu cannot be compared. The one is surrounded by cultivated parks and thriving modern cities, the other with the abandon of nature. Niagara makes a single leap over a precipice one hundred and eighty feet high, while Iguazu is broken in fall but far wider. Either one is a possession for any country to be proud of and neither one is worth a single quarrel.

"We are to camp here for some days. I hope you little folk will have a nice time and I am not going to issue a lot of commands to spoil your pleasure. Only one thing is forbidden; you must never go away from camp without one of the servants unless you are with one of us grown people. Do you understand?"

"Yes, sir," they all said, and he added,

"I am sure I can trust you. The forest is full of all manner of animals and creeping things, and it would be very easy to lose your way, so that we could never find you again. Now, have all the fun you can for our week here will soon be over."

What orgies of delight followed! The girls bathed in the stream and ran wild in the sunshine, happy and tanned, going into the forest with the boys, except when they were going hunting.

Several days before their return home, the whole party went up to San Ignacio to see the ruins of the old mission in the heart of the woods. Huge trees mark the site of the flourishing town, where once were cheerful homes which only eighty years ago were burned. So well were these dwellings built that the ruins are in excellent preservation, and the children played hide-and-seek in and out of the deserted walls, their merry laughter waking the echoes of the past. Maria had taught them the game she called 'High Spy,' and they enjoyed it greatly, she most of all.

"Now then, Martim, it's your turn to be it," she said. "And you can't find me!" as she sped away to hide in some new and strange place. Before she knew it she had gone farther into the forest than she meant, and she did not know how to return. She turned this way and that, but there seemed no path. All about her the woods hemmed her in everywhere like a great green curtain. Then catching her foot in a swinging vine she fell and hurt her ankle. Frightened, she stood under a great magnolia to think.

"I must not be silly and cry," she said to herself. "I can't have gone very far, and if I sit still they'll be sure to come and find me. If I go on I may just get farther and farther away. I am going to stay right here anyway, until my ankle is better," as she seated herself quietly.

Maria was a brave child and old for her age, and she sat quite still, though the tears came into her eyes.

Soon she grew very drowsy and could hardly keep awake, for the woods were full of soft, cooing sounds and at last she dropped asleep.

It was almost twilight when she awoke, and the rays of the setting sun gleamed between the leaves. Drowsily stirring, she heard the sound of voices, and sitting up suddenly she saw a little Indian girl talking to a splendid cockatoo which perched upon her hand. The parrot was chattering in Portuguese, and his little mistress was talking to him lovingly, but she sprang away in fright as Maria got up from the ground.

"Can you show me the way to the camp?" she asked. "I am lost."

"What camp? Where did you come from?" asked the Indian. She was a little younger than Maria, and dressed in a quaint little peasant's costume of blue skirt and red blouse with a huge straw hat upon her black hair.

Quickly Maria told her story and the little girl said,

"I can take you back. You must have run very quickly to have come so far. We must start at once to reach the Mission before dark."

"Oh, thank you ever so much," said Maria. "I am so anxious to get back, for my father will be hunting for me."

"He might hunt all night and not find you, for the forest has many paths," said the little girl. She had a sad little face but it was very sweet when she smiled.

"What is your name?" asked Maria as the two girls trudged along through the forest, her companion still carrying the cockatoo.

"Guacha, because I have no mother," she answered. "That is my Indian name, but I am also called Teresa."

"My mother is dead, too," said Maria, and the two little girls looked into one another's eyes with sympathy.

"My father is dead, also," said Guacha. "We were of the Mission Indians, but all my own people died of the fever two years ago."

"But who do you live with?" asked Maria. "Have you no friends at all?"

"Oh, I live with some of the Indians who were my father's friends!" said Guacha, "and Chiquita here is my good friend," and she smiled at the bird, who chattered to her gaily and pecked gently at her cheek. "I wish you could go home with me!" cried Maria impulsively, and just then she heard a shout resounding through the forest,

"Maria! Maria!" sounded her father's voice, and the two little girls hurried along faster, Maria answering the call as loudly as she could.

In a few moments they came in sight of the camp, and Maria was caught to her father's breast and kissed and scolded all in the same breath, while the rest of the children gathered around, eager with questions, all but Guacha, who stood apart, wistful and silent. Maria did not forget her, however, for escaping from her father's arms, she took the little Indian girl by the hand and said,

"Scold me all you want to, Daddy, though I did not mean to run away, but be kind to Guacha, who brought me back and who has no father."

Then the little Indian was made welcome, thanked and made much of, and the Senhora said,

"You must stay all night with us, dear child, for it is too late for you to return home through the forest. Will they be worried about you?"

"Thank you, Senhora, I will stay," she said simply. "There is no one at all to worry about me."

CHAPTER XII

GUACHA

CHIQUITA and Guacha proved a pleasant addition to the happy circle of little folk, for, though shy at first, the little Indian soon thawed out in the genial atmosphere about her. Many quaint little stories she told of Indian ways and customs, legends of the times of the Inca conquests, and stories of the days when her forefathers had been Caciques of the tribe. She was a sweet-natured little soul, and the Senhora kept her with them until the last day of their stay.

The evening before they were to return to Sao Paulo, all sat around the camp-fire, laughing, talking, and telling stories, Guacha beside Maria, for the two little girls had grown nearly inseparable. The green and red cockatoo was perched upon Guacha's shoulder, half asleep, but when his little mistress laughed, he chuckled sleepily, that half amused, half contemptuous laugh which makes a parrot seem so human.

"To-morrow we start toward home," said Lola dreamily, as she sat resting her head against her mother's knee.

"Saudade, little daughter?" asked her father.

"Oh, no, papa, how could I be really homesick when I am having such a delightful time with my cousins," said Lola sweetly. "But I should like to see grandmamma in Para and my dear old nurse at the fazenda."

"I want to see Joachim and Vicente," said Affonzo.

"I want to see mamma," said Martim. Big boy that he was, he was not ashamed of being devoted to his mother.

Maria's eyes filled with tears, and she slipped one hand into her father's and he held it tight.

The Senhora hummed lightly under her breath the sweet Brazilian "Home Sweet Home," then the young folk took up the strain and sang together:

"Mine is the country where the palm-trees rear

Their stately heads toward the azure sky,

And where, in accents ever soft and clear,

The sabiá sings her hymn of melody;

Here, in my exile, say what warblers rare

Can with the sabiá's notes their own compare?

"Friendless, alone, at night, I dream of thee;

My slumbering senses wrapped in peace and bliss

I see the palms; the sabiá's melody

Falls on my ears; once more I feel the kiss

Of lips I love; I wake, the vision's gone,

The sabiá to his native woods has flown.

"Spare me, O God, until in peace I lie

Asleep for ever in the land I love,

Then may the sabiá carol joyfully,

Perched in the palms, my resting-place above.

So gathering in the first-fruits of my love,

No longer homesick, every heart-ache past,

Bearing the sheaves for which in grief I strove,

A plenteous harvest may I reap at last."

As they finished, Maria heard from the slight figure beside her a sigh that was almost a sob and she turned quickly to find Guacha's eyes filled with tears, fixed upon her.

"What is it?" she whispered. "Are you ill?"

"Oh no," said Guacha. "But you all love each other so dearly and I have no one to love, only Chiquita," as the cockatoo rubbed his fluffy head against her cheek.

"You have me," said Maria.

"But you are going away from me," she answered mournfully.

"No, my child." Maria's father laid his hand kindly upon the little Indian's dark head. "You may come with us if you will."

"Oh, papa!" cried Maria, her face alight with eager delight. "Will you really take Guacha back with us?"

"I thought that you might like to have her go back with us and play that she was your sister," he said pleasantly. "Your aunt says she will take care of you both during the rest of the year, and the old people who have cared for your little friend are ready to give her to us if she wants to come. How about it, Guacha? Will you go far off to Para and be Guacha's sister?"

She looked from him to Maria, from Maria to the Senhora, who smiled at her kindly.

"May I take Chiquita?" she asked. "He hasn't a friend in all the world but me."

"Of course you may take your birdie, you dear little girl," said the Senhora, "and we shall all hope to have you very happy with us."

Guacha gave a contented little sigh, and slipped her hand into Maria's.

"You are all so good," she said. "I could never be anything but happy with you."

"It will be ever so jolly," broke out Affonzo, the irrepressible.

"Yes," said Martim. "I'll have another girl cousin to tease, but she won't treat me as unkindly as you treat your Brazilian cousins, Maria."

"Well, maybe not," laughed Maria, "but you know Guacha is the only one of you all who is really and truly my Little Brazilian Cousin."

THE END.

Milton Keynes UK
Ingram Content Group UK Ltd.
UKHW021943160724
445389UK00010B/486